Sto[illegible]
2008

HappenStance

ISBN 978-1-905939-16-9

Acknowledgements:
Thanks to Susie Maguire for her generous support in reading, judging and helping to promote this year's competition. Thanks also to competition administrator Sarah Willans, without whom (yet again) none of this would have been possible.

Published by Happen*Stance*
21 Hatton Green, Glenrothes,
Fife KY7 4SD
www.happenstancepress.com

Orders
Further copies available for £3.00 (including UK p&p).
Please make cheques payable to Happen*Stance*
or order through PayPal on the website.
Further information: nell@happenstancepress.com

Contents

Seeing Anyone

Tom Vowler

Today stretches out before me like some vast desert I don't want to cross. The drive north to her house feels slow, somehow uphill, as if the car is subject to the earth's curvature. Choosing what to listen to is impossible: there is no music for this, so the last hundred miles pass in silence.

And then suddenly I'm there, pulling into an unfamiliar driveway, in front of a cottage I'd pictured differently, with a garden we'd once dreamt of together. I turn the engine off, exhale deeply and now that it's too late, ask myself if I should have come. Then she's standing there, smiling, as if I pop round each day. I pick up the envelope of photographs and the thirsty tiger lilies and step out.

'Hey, you,' Sarah says.

'Hey.'

We hug clumsily. I wait for the musk of Chanel to hit me, but it doesn't.

'You look well,' I say. 'Must be the country air.'

'You, too. Come on, come in.'

Following her inside, I'm unable to resist a glance at a finger on her left hand, which I see is bare.

Some of the furniture is familiar. A radio offers benign jazz that's barely audible. Smells compete for my attention: pungent ash from a recent fire, vinegary pickles and chutney waft in from the kitchen, and the thick sweet scent of the oak beams, strewn throughout, the grain full of secrets and memories.

'Here, let me put those in some water.'

'Wasn't sure what to bring...'

'They're beautiful. She's in the garden, under the tree. Coffee?'

The tree is a crab apple, offering mottled shade. Curled up beneath it, on a worn tartan blanket, is Millie. I've not seen her for three years. She hears me coming and tries to bark a warning but is too weak. Then she recognises me, by my smell or face or voice, I'm not sure, and her tail beats slowly against the ground. She tries to get up but I hurry to her. I can't believe how old she looks. Much of her coat is grey and matted; her legs are like knotted sticks, her face gaunt. I stroke her head and she lifts it into my hand. As I move my face nearer her, there's a smell I can't quite place—fetid and otherworldly, like death.

'The drugs make her stomach bloat like that,' Sarah says, handing me the coffee, a mug with a cow on it that I'd drunk from in another lifetime. She sits on the wooden bench next to us.

'Is Pete...?'

'He's away,' she says. 'A golf weekend.'

I flash a curious, almost judgemental look—golf!—and for a moment she indulges me before looking away, perhaps feeling disloyal. I consider whether his absence changes the essence of my visit, whether I'll stay longer, whether we'll veer from small talk.

'Poor thing,' I say, turning back to Millie, who manages another wag. 'Wasn't sure she'd remember me.'

'They do.'

'What's the vet said?'

A few days, probably. I have to decide when enough's enough for her really, and not be selfish about it.'

'She's no age at all.'

'I didn't know whether to tell you. I thought about it for days.'

'I'm glad you did.'

A warm breeze weaves between us, carrying a small flower from the cherry blossom in the far corner. It catches in the strands of her hair like confetti, offering itself to me. I start to move my hand but it blows away.

For the first time I absorb the fragrance and colour around me, wondering if she's its sole architect, or if Pete has a say. The beds, I know are hers. Chillies and radishes, peppers and tomatoes, stretch upwards, the last of the morning dew shimmering against the profusion of vermillion and green and ochre. A decked area is festooned with stone and marble pots. I recognise the two peach trees that were a tenth the size when I loaded them into the back of Pete's van in that other time. I'd asked to keep one, but she said they mated with each other and needed to be close, which only made me love her more. I remember looking hard at her that day, trying to see if all her love for me had left, like a distant star that's seen but is no longer there.

'How've you been, Steve?' she says without looking up. I try to process whether the use of my name is intimate. It feels like a wall.

'Good. Yeah, good, really. You?'

'Things are good, really working out. We had to re-mortgage last year when I got laid off, but we're picking ourselves up. You still teaching?'

'Gave up...'

'God, what...?'

'Bought some Canadian canoes, me and Shaun take groups down the Tamar. This is our second season.'

'I can't believe you did it. I mean, well done. That's great.'

'Not had a headache since.'

'Pete's business is starting to take off. He says this time next year...' She trails off, leans forward in her chair and gently loops some hair on Millie's tummy round a finger. Our exchange, anodyne and synthetic, both surprises me yet is expected: the Doppler effect of love, where sound and language differ so much depending on whether it's arriving or departing.

Some words appear in my mind and are betrayed by my vocal cords: 'You're happy?'

'Mmm, yeah, of course. Why wouldn't I be?'

'Sorry, I just meant...'

We both play with the rim of our cups for a while.

I wait till her face softens, then: 'I brought these, don't know if you want to see them.'

She takes the envelope and starts to look through photographs of the first four years of Millie's life. 'I don't remember any of these.'

'We took so many.'

I let her study them without interruption, content to watch the emotions flicker across her face. By the end there's an ambivalence in her eyes, as if I've dragged us back through time. She recovers and hands them back with a smile I'd almost forgotten.

'I can copy any you want,' I say.

'That'd be nice.'

'Do you remember how we chose her?' She does, of course, but plays along anyway by not answering. 'That farm outside Totnes. The puppies were curled up at the back of a pig sty, sleeping. They all rushed to us, but then started to play with each other. Millie was the only one who stayed and nibbled our hands.'

'I preferred the markings on the other one, but you wouldn't hear of it,' she says.

Again I steal a longer look at her and notice how much older her face looks. It could still take all the air from a man, but I realise how photographs and the memory keep the face at the age you last saw it, preserved as if in amber. I remember I used to think her beauty wasn't an obvious one, that you had to let it unfurl into your heart over time. But when truly seen, like a shape hidden within an optical illusion, you could see nothing else.

'Are you seeing anyone, then?' she says, looking down at the grass.

The question jolts me and seems to resound inside my head. Noticing my hesitation, she apologises.

'No, it's fine. Not really, no.' I'm used to giving this answer to my parents, to friends. They'll tease me, goad me to expand on the 'not really', but today it just ushers in a silence, which I break with: 'I'm happy, though.'

The homemade soup is like visiting my childhood home, its flavours awakening long-suppressed images and feelings. The only noise above the music is the occasional clinking of spoon on bowl and the breaking of bread. I wonder whether she feels awkward in the silence, but neither of us fills it.

Back outside, we return to the safety of unremarkable words—of respective families and old friends, innocuous anecdotes and world events. And then, as if by some trick of time, the shadows are lengthening and I'm getting up to go.

I kiss Millie on the side of the head. 'Will you let me know when...?'

'Of course,' Sarah says.

We hug and I'm sure the perfume of her skin and hair, of *her*, will crush me. I go to pull away but she holds on. Observed from a distance, it would go unnoticed, yet just by tensing her arms she seems to change everything. I wonder how many moments make a life and whether this eclipses all of them. I want to freeze the action. *Say something, for fuck's sake. Find some words.* But I don't.

Behind her, I take a last look at the cottage, their home, for a second allowing myself to traverse reality. I picture myself in an upstairs window, watching as she tends the garden like a sculptor, the seasons wrapping us with their certainty as we age together, suffused in love. Of all heaven's gifts, imagination is the cruellest.

She sees me out onto the road, the crunch of gravel deafening and damning. In the space between reversing and setting off, our eyes meet. No smiles, no words.

Are you in love? If so, how much? Do you ever look at pictures of me? What are you reading? Why did you leave? What is it that joins people? Where does it go? Could we... Could...

We don't wave. I look at her in my mirror watching to see if my brake lights come on. Out of sight, the tears begin to burn in my eyes.

Wrong Bus

Jo Field

THE REASON HE'S on the wrong bus is sitting three seats in front of him. Her hair is tugged back quite harshly in a copper-coloured ponytail, except it hasn't been fully pulled through the loop, so that it is itself a loop: thick, with the ends sticking up in a Hiawatha feather-effect towards the top of her head. In the groove down the back of her neck lies a loosely curled strand, a tendril. The temptation to lean right forward and blow at it, try to stir it, to watch the bounce of it, is very great. When she turns her head to look out of the window, he is presented with the profile which first claimed his attention, more Modigliani than Botticelli: long nose with a swoop to it, small silver-studded ear, fragile chin.

When we look at someone long and hard, perhaps we subtract a piece of that person. It could be the same with mere objects. Who knows—it may be that we steal a tiny facet of another dimension of the object or the person, in order to pack it away in our memory. Perhaps it might work in the very way that causes some to fear the camera: those people who think it will suck out their soul. The girl feels his stare. She feels it as theft, he can tell. With difficulty, he shifts his eyes away as she turns on him the back of her head.

The day before yesterday the wrong bus came by. He was standing at the stop waiting, none too patiently, for the right one, when another drew up. Exactly in front of him, as if deliberately manoeuvred into place, the girl's profile halted. He couldn't help but look. When she turned her head and met his eyes with her own, wide and just a little indignant; when her small full mouth gathered itself together in displeasure as she turned quickly away, then a sharp shaft of something red hot seemed to bury itself in his chest.

He didn't think of moving, almost forgot to breathe, until the bus pulled away, Then foolishly he chased along the pavement, at first beside, then behind it, before juddering to a halt and walking slowly back, self-conscious once more, to rejoin the indifferent queue at the bus stop. For the rest of the day he cursed himself mercilessly for his stupor and, when night finally arrived, he took the words *if only* to bed with him and hugged them, with all their permutations, in his wakeful brain.

The next day—yesterday—one hour earlier than the encounter of the day before, he set up his surveillance at the bus stop in front of the florist's. Every Number 74 was subjected to his anxious scrutiny, and every 30 and 52 as well. The occasional double-decker he greeted with despair. He toyed with the idea of leaping on and up and down and out, but quailed at the thought of explaining himself to the driver, and at the sight of passengers poised judgemental in their seats. His hopes, his expectations see-sawed, either sky-high or jolted out of him altogether as they hit the mud. Other queuers ebbed and flowed around him. After two hours and ten minutes, tasting the bitter dust of disappointment all the way to his stomach, he gave up.

Except that he didn't give up. Why should she have been delivered to him, literally face to face? Why should the sight of her have affected him as a blow to the solar plexus? Why indeed if it were not *meant to be*? He sat in the window of a café overlooking the pavement where the buses stopped. After each cup was drained to the froth, he ventured out yet again, a desperate Galahad on a wild grail chase. He phoned in sick, not caring that the comings and goings of a public place could be easily discerned behind his lies. When it was as dark as it was going to be, he went home.

Confined, solitary in his room, he sat and stared at the carpet. The patch under his feet where the pile was worn away was in the shape of a heart: not a valentine heart, but one from a school textbook, with its atriums and ventricles and its rude tubes projecting, superior and inferior. He rubbed his bare feet over it, bent to pick up a button and a small piece of toast, dropped them again and kicked them under the sofa. He made an urgent picture behind his eyes of the little ear with its stud of silver in the lobe, then of the little mouth, delicately puckered. He felt that same sharp darting heat, but lower down, in his loins; and he visualized the aridity there as a desert.

In all honesty, this was the worst it had ever been Never—he thought back hastily—no *never* had the feeling been so strong. He stood, and unhooked the faded Matisse print of 'Bathers with a Turtle' from the wall above the television. He examined it for the first time in a while. Rather than revelling in its serenity, he saw now how the naked girls were teasing the creature; how one of them sniggered behind her hand. He looked in the fridge for beer, made do with the miniature of brandy he hadn't used on his Christmas pudding. Later, he trussed himself into bed like a mummy and lay stiff and still for many hours.

The following day—today—he reached the bus stop earlier than before. He leant his back against the wall of the florist's shop, one foot braced against the bricks. Between buses he examined his bent knee, the white threads holding together the blue of the frayed denim; the way they stretched across the pale skin underneath, just biting into the flesh. The florist kept coming out with buckets and sheaves of garish flowers. He avoided her curious glances.

And then the miracle. The wrong bus, transformed in a drench of sudden magic into the right one. Inside his chest grows a lump of joy, a balloon the size of the future, as he floats along the aisle towards her.

Where to sit? The other half of her seat is empty, but then so are many other seats all around. He has no wish to presume; no desire to crowd her. As he loiters past she looks briefly at his face. Her eyes, he sees, are darker than he thought. There seems to be no glint of recognition as he tries to load his soul into a smile. She looks out of the window. He chooses the third seat behind her and sits on the edge.

He should have bought flowers. Nothing over the top, a small spray of those scented bell-things—freesias?—perhaps. He could have presented them in passing, with an apt throw-away line. He gropes for the throw-away line he might have used, but it eludes him. Dumbly, he watches the bob and spring of the strand of Titian hair, soft on the neck in front of him as she turns her face to and from the window. When she stands to get off the bus, again he almost forgets to move from his trance.

Shuffling back along the aisle, hanging a few decorous paces behind, he has the chance to observe the whole of her for the first time. Mildly, he is surprised. He has pictured her tall, in some sort of flowing Bohemian garb, Pre-Raphaelite robes perhaps, with the shape of her body just discernible, fine and small-boned. Rather, she seems fairly short, wearing tight black jeans and a dark blue jacket which swings as she walks and shows off her her overlarge behind. He doesn't mind that she strides out mannishly; and a big bottom's fine by him. He follows her down from the step, his brain busy with the necessary adjustments.

She hovers by the back of the bus, waiting for a lull in the traffic. It's a silly place to cross the road and he frowns, a frown prompted partly by concern, partly by irritation. But his forehead relaxes as that profile of hers turns right to left to right, an obedient child observing the Green Cross Code. He stands at her shoulder, as close as he dares. Yes, the top of her head reaches only to his chin, more vulnerable than if it were higher. She notices him there and, with a flounce, yes a real *flounce*, retreats to the pavement and starts to walk away.

He lets her go on ahead. He doesn't want to spook her. Then he picks up the trail, lingering behind the cover of fellow pedestrians, occasionally turning to a shop window, the way he's seen it done in the movies. She marches purposefully, block after block, her outsize bag like a sack nudging at her hip, the loose strand of hair bouncing, that profile appearing and vanishing as she angles her head from side to side. She has an artistic streak, he reckons. She's so obviously interested in everything that goes on around her. It pleases him when they both notice, at the same time, the scaffolder at the corner who swings his dangling legs as he casually turns a page of his book.

Again, she wants to cross the road. Again she chooses a stupid place to do it, between two parked cars, when there's plenty of space beyond them. Again he frowns. This time irritation wins out over concern. He stops behind her. *What do you think you're doing?* he wants to say. Again she notices his presence behind her, and she turns towards him.

'What do you think you're doing?' It's she who says it. 'You're following me, aren't you?'

Her voice has an aggressive edge that jars. He reaches out to her in a gesture which is mostly defensive.

People talk about a *squeal* of brakes. It's not a squeal, exactly, this noise. It's more percussive, and entirely shocking. It ends with a gentle thud like a drumbeat muffled with sacking. The car has come to a halt, slewed against one of those parked at the kerb. Dropped into the silence like a pebble in a pond is a sharp sob, before the world gets going again. She is sitting in the road; the driver of the car is bending over her; other people stand around with mobile phones.

'He *pushed* me.'

One of her arms looks limp and awkward. The other points accusingly. Faces turn towards him. The driver and another man help her gingerly to her feet. Someone brings a chair from the nearest shop and she is eased on to it. She seems to have lost something. In her white face, the eyes search wildly about her.

'My bag,' she says. 'Where's my bag?' Even in extremis, her voice has that belligerent grate to it.

He catches sight of the bag lying in the road. It looks flat and crumpled, as if it has borne the brunt of the impact.

'What are you doing with that?' someone asks him as he stands with the bag's carcass in his hands. Somebody snatches it away and reunites it with its owner.

And somebody else lays a firm hand on his arm and says: '*Did* you push her?'

The Hour

Hannah Eiseman-Renyard

I stand outside his door, staring at my watch. Two minutes to go. I can hear the bells, laughter and muffled audience applause of a TV quiz show inside the house.

One minute to go.

For a moment I wonder if this is really necessary, but watching the seconds scroll down from forty to twenty, I remember just how many times he's kept me awake with the relentless thumping bass of his music. How many times he's filled both his wheelie bin and mine with a backlog of rubbish, stranding me with two weeks' worth of stinking bin bags in the summer heat. Yes, I really *do* want to do this.

1:00 AM. Go.

The doorbell is an angry buzzer. Thirty seconds pass. I hear him lumbering to the door.

'Hey, Brian, what can I d—'

My fist—spring-loaded—darts straight for his jaw. It isn't my choice any more, isn't my fault. My arm just wanted it. His head ricochets back with the blow and I'm off.

'What the hell?' He starts a heavy pace towards me, but I'm already running. 'Hey, come back here, you little shit!' I'm out of his reach, and he gives up the chase. 'You think you'll get away with this, you fucking faggot? I know where you fucking live!' he bellows after me, his voice getting further and further away as I sprint down the darkened street.

I know, I know: not the most diplomatic way to deal with a problem neighbour. What the hell am I doing? This will only hit me back and harder, right? But it's okay, I've got this all under control; he won't remember a thing in the morning. Hell, he won't remember it in fifty-eight minutes.

Next stop is seven blocks away. My feet slam down on each paving stone. Fifty-six minutes and twenty seconds. I sprint across the bright petrol station forecourt, with its rack of newspapers and bucket of lacklustre flowers. I grab a bunch with a rose at the centre and zip left, out of the light.

I rip apart the cellophane as I go, shedding all other contents. Baby's breath, salmon pink carnations, magenta chrysanthemums: I leave a trail of botanical carnage. All I need is the one red rose. The houses become progressively taller as I go, the gardens better maintained. Glimpses through lighted windows start revealing small sculptures and 'ethnic' artefacts on windowsills. Welcome to the middle-class part of town.

One block to go and I've barely broken a sweat. Are you impressed? I do hope so. I've been working out for this.

This front door has a stained glass panel and the doorbell is a twee ascending three-tone. She answers with a glass of red wine almost dangling from her long fingers. The mellow scent of cooking rice wafts out of the house.

'Hello.'

'Hello, Samantha. Remember me?' Okay, I am panting a little, and she's looking pretty freaked. Her free hand goes behind the door, about to push it shut, but I wedge my foot in there first. 'I was going to be your date to the cinema—on Valentine's Day, when we were sixteen, remember? —but you stood me up.'

Her expression slackens before her face contorts in a whole new way; eyes widen and her mouth opens, searching for words, like a fish gasping in a net.

'No, don't worry, you don't have to say anything. I just wanted to give you this—'

The stalk whips across her face with a satisfying flex. A single scarlet petal flutters to her doormat.

Bitch-slapped with a rose. It seemed appropriate.

Forty-eight minutes left.

Okay, I know, I've lost you. But what you don't get is that no one will remember this come one o'clock. Or, rather, the second one o'clock. Y'see, tonight's the night that the clocks go back.

The silhouette of a cat skitters across the road. I'm starting to feel the sprint: not tired yet, but getting warmer.

But yes, where was I? Ah, one o'clock. It's simple. So unbelievably simple it's almost stupid. See the hour between 1:00AM and 1:00AM, when the clocks go back, doesn't actually exist. Poetic, isn't it? But this isn't just some daylight saving technicality: it *really* doesn't exist.

Forty-one minutes. The gravel path crackles underfoot. God, it took me ages to find out where this guy lives. It feels so good to stop for a moment. I gasp for breath and undo my flies. Forty minutes. I ring the doorbell and do up my zip. He answers bleary-eyed, in worn pyjamas.

'Uh, hi?'

'Hello, you're the guy that always gives me a dirty look on the bus.'

'What?' He winces in the light of his own hallway. 'Sorry?'

'You give me a dirty look on the bus almost every day. I don't know why you do it. It's nasty and unnecessary and generally ruins my day. Anyway, I've just pissed in your letterbox.'

'What?' His eyes widen ever so slightly.

'Right there. See that wet bit on your doormat? I did that.'

'Why would you—'

'Bye!'

I'm off down the street again. By the end of the block I've hit my stride, and I savour the stretch in the backs of my thighs with each lunge.

Two more streets. They're long, but it's all downhill. My legs whir under me, almost without thought, it goes so easily. Thirty-three minutes. The hour is nearly half-way through.

For the last three years I've been up at this hour; recording it, proving it, making sure. The first two years it was just a boring recording of me walking about in my flat, making cups of tea and watching TV (always the news, with the 24-hour clock in the bottom corner. Proof.) In the morning I remembered *planning* it, and I always had the recording, but I had no memories of the actual hour. Last year I invited friends around and filmed us all, to check if it was just me, but it was everyone: no-one remembered anything we'd done for those sixty minutes. They all agreed that was strange—they hadn't drunk *that* much. Then they shrugged and opened another six-pack of beer.

I round the corner. An overgrown hedge catches me unawares. Leaves bombard my face and twigs tear across my shoulder as I rush past. At the end of the block are the chipboard walls of the building site.

This hour exists when you're in it, you can do normal things in it: if you drop a plate in that hour, the plate will still be smashed after, but you never remember the actual events of the hour. Think—can you remember what you did, in this one limbo hour, last time the clocks went back?

I didn't think so.

So, here it is, ticking smaller by the second. Thirty minutes. Already half-way through the hour that doesn't count; my marathon of scot-free amusement and petty acts of revenge. Wouldn't you, if you knew you could?

I near the building site. I stick my arm in the second to last hedge, the one with the variegated privet, and grope about for the torch and axe I stashed there this afternoon. Be prepared, and all that. Twenty-nine minutes left. I cross the road. The first axe-swing is a little off-centre and only flakes at the plywood, but the second does the trick: splinters fringe the hole, and the padlock clunks to the pavement. I zip inside, round the back of the CCTV camera. I'm scanning the shadows for the safety cage, vertical hydraulics and the dinky little wheels. Got it! There's the forklift truck.

Hotwiring takes a little while. My fingers shake with the adrenaline; I'm panting something chronic, and holding the torch in place under my chin, struggling to keep the light pointed where I want it.

Sorted. *Go.* Twenty-two minutes.

There's something ridiculous about the speed of a forklift truck. Like trying to get excited about a milkfloat.

Twenty-one minutes.

Only a few windows are lighted on the whole street. I feel sorry for all the suckers who are asleep now, or just watching one more hour of forgettable TV. Just think what they could do if they were making their hour really count.

Residential streets aren't made for forklift trucks. A late night dog walker stiffens up as I lumber closer. I grin a big cheesy daytime TV smile at him, and wave. He looks away, but I see him peering after me in the wing mirrors once I've passed. This is the street. He drives a Mercedes with a sandy gold paint job, but under orange streetlights I can't tell 'sandy' from 'silver.' Eighteen minutes. What the hell is his licence plate?

Ah, there it is! Traffic cones marking his spot, the ostentatious bastard. I turn the forklift to face it side-on and lower the prongs. A little closer. Seventeen minutes. And raise them. The forklift is so strong I can't feel the weight of the load. I just watch, passive, as the car in front of me lifts, tilts and crunches loudly to its side. I drive forward, pushing it just a few more inches and it tilts further, wobbles, and falls, upside-down onto the pavement.

The crash echoes down the street. Dogs bark, lights turn on. I get out and walk to number eighty-one.

My boss's door flings open before I've rung the bell. His comb-over is dishevelled and I really hope it's his wife's pink dressing gown he's in.

'What the hell was— Brian, is that you? What in goodness' name are you doing here?'

'Just flipping your car.'

'I beg your pardon?'

'Your car. You gave yourself a raise while cutting employee pay. So I flipped your car.'

He runs barefoot to where his baby lies like a giant, stranded beetle. The doors are crumpled where it dropped on its side, the back passenger window is in thousands of tiny, icy cubes. Fourteen minutes. 'You're fired! You're prosecuted! You're a dead man—d'you hear me?'

I walk towards him. The comb-over has fallen down, it's just one hank of hair, dangling off one side of his shiny, bald head. God, I've been wanting to do this since my first day at work: I pull out a hanky, and buff at his head in small, circular motions. 'Beautiful shine you've got.'

He flails at me, but I'm already running. Thirteen minutes. I sprint two streets away, out of earshot and eyeshot, and take out my phone. I dial Amy, and pull out a crumpled sheet of paper.

1. punch Tom
2. hit Samantha with a flower
3. piss in bus guy's letterbox
4. total boss's car
5. ring Amy

It's ringing. She'd better pick up.

I cross out the first four. This hour doesn't just work for everyone else; it works for me too: I'm not going to remember a thing. All I have is these sixty minutes, and this checked-off list that will tell me I managed everything I'd planned.

She picks up, her words slurred with sleep. 'Brian? What's up, sweetie? You woke me up.'

'Hey Amy, I just wanted to say how much I love you.'

She makes a little moan, like she does when she rolls over in the night. 'I love you too, babe, but it's nearly two in the morning.'

'Not really.'

Eleven minutes.

'What?'

'Nothing. Amy, listen: I love you, I don't ever want there to be anyone else. I only want you. Forever.'

She giggles. 'How much have you had?'

'None, Amy, I've just been doing some thinking.'

'Okay babe, but how about you come round in the morning? I've got some of that fancy cereal you like and—'

'Marry me, Amy.'

There's a pause. A silence. A big silence. Oh God, what's she thinking? My phone bleeps. The screen reads BATTERY LOW, then goes blank.

Holy shitting crap! Ten minutes left and she's on the other side of town. I have to know. It'll be another year before I can find out if she'd say 'yes.' I sprint so fast you'd swear my legs were mechanised. Nine minutes left. Nine goddamn minutes!

Down Park Lane, up Oak Place. Across the empty main road. Through the little back roads to the highroad. Left at the corner shop and I'm on her road. Two minutes left.

It's uphill. My throat burns as I gasp and lunge, but I've got to know. I ring her doorbell. One minute and twenty seconds left.

She answers the door, looking like she might cry. 'Why did you hang up? I kept trying to call you.'

'I didn't—hang up—' I pant. 'My phone—phone battery went dead.'

'Oh my God, did you run all the way?' She breaks into the kind of smile that just kills me—the creases radiate from her eyes. 'Come here.' She reaches her arms out and I snuggle my cheek down into her hair, kiss the top of her head. I could just stay here forever. But the hour. I open one eye enough to check my watch.

Twenty seconds.

'So what's your answer? Will you?'

She giggles in my arms. 'Don't be silly.'

'Silly? I'm not kidding Amy. Will you marry me?'

'I told you on the phone, babe.'

'My phone battery died on me! I didn't hear! Tell me, will you marry me?' My voice is loud, high, desperate. Five seconds left.

'Whoa.' She breaks apart and looks me in the eye. 'Brian, what's the rush? It's not like there's some time limi—'

Zero seconds.

In the Constitution

Joel Willans

WHEN I GOT the Oakland greyhound to San Fran, the bus was full of dwarfs. I know that sounds crazy as hell, but I'm not kidding you. Every single goddamn person on that bus besides me and the driver was a little guy. They were squealing and squeaking and jumping around. I kept my head down and went way up back, all the time wondering what kind of fix I'd got myself into.

Don't get me wrong; it wasn't that I had anything personal against them. I wouldn't have wanted to shack up with one, or take one to the game, but they're human beings too, right? I mean it's in the Constitution. There in black and white. *Equal before God. Big and small.* But a whole busload of them. That was just way over-the-top freaky for a small town guy like me.

So anyways, after an hour or so, I started to get real paranoid, like it wasn't them that were small but me who was frigging tall. I wiped the dirt off the back window so I could make sure that the whole world hadn't gone dwarf, but we were in the middle of nowhere, just desert as far as you could see. Then I started panicking, getting hold of my gear and sliding down my chair so I wouldn't seem such a damn giant.

I checked my watch and we had at least three more hours until we got to the city. I'd never been to San Fran before, but now all the stuff people said back home started filling my head. What if the dwarfs weren't just small but fags, too? Christ, I thought, what if they were sadomasochists and wanted to nail me to a plank of wood or something? I rummaged through my bag to see what I could use as a weapon if they came for me. Zip. Not even a pen to poke their little eyes out with.

I punched the seat, cussing myself for not listening to Pops when he told me I should get some firepower. Nothing fancy, he said, just a little Browning or a Colt. He'd heard the stories. He remembered the sixties. Better safe than sorry, just in case it got a bit crazy down there. Well, it didn't get much crazier than riding through the desert with a busload of lollipop kids.

Paranoia, it's a goddamn killer. Truly. I'm young, I'm fit and I reckoned I could take at least four, maybe five, but not twenty. So I kept on thinking how, if things got nasty, I'm a goner. The thought made my stomach clench like my insides had done a runner and my body was trying to hide it. When the bus pulled into a gas station, I bundled my way off as fast as a shark. I needed to breathe. I needed big space. But I was too damn quick. I flew down them steps so fast that I hit the ground running. Then boom, two, three strides and I went headlong into this fat trucker climbing down off his rig. The back of his big old head bounced off his door, and he fell flat on his face.

'Jees, I'm sorry, buddy,' I said. 'I didn't mean no harm. I didn't see ya.'

Real slow, he pulled himself off the floor and dusted himself down and all I could do was stare at his hands. They were like two joints of ham, and though I'm no mind reader, I could tell I was in for some serious pain. He frowned at me, and his brow went so low it squished his eyes into his head.

'You some clown, ain't ya?' he spat. 'Saying you couldn't see me, are ya? Is that what ya saying, boy?'

I smelt him then. Sweat and gasoline and tacos all came bowling towards me like a gust of foul wind.

I shook my head. 'Yes, sir, I was just saying that...'

He grabbed my shirt and wrenched me closer, and I started thinking goddamn if he ain't going to eat me. Instead, he pulled back a fist the size of a baby's head and I wished I'd never, ever left Rockford. Just then, as I waited for the pain with my eyes crunched up, I heard a racket of small voices.

'What you think you're doing?

'Leave him be.'

'It was an accident, big guy.'

Next thing I knew, the trucker dumped my ass in the dust, and stood glaring at the dwarfs. They were circling him, waving their fists and I wondered what the hell they were playing at. One with slick-back Elvis hair had a real big mouth on him and he shouted all these taunts, stirring up the trucker like a rodeo clown teasing a mean old bull. It worked real good, too. The trucker swung at him and just when it looked like this baby rocker was gonna get his head knocked clean off, he did this backward-roll trick, leaving the trucker's fist flying through thin air.

The trucker bellowed and I shouted out for some help, but my voice was lost in the hollering and before I could say another thing, the dwarfs were bouncing and spinning and flying through the frigging air and the trucker was on the floor and they were jumping on his gut like it was a trampoline. When he was good and quiet, they clambered off and Elvis grabbed the trucker's fat face between his chubby fingers.

'Next time, Bud, pick on someone your own size,' he said.

The trucker nodded and the little guys waddled back onto the bus, one by one. I got up, and dammit I was almost crying, so choked up I was that these tiny fellas had come and helped me out when they might just as well have watched me getting all smacked up. I stumbled back on the bus and stood up front near the driver.

'Hey guys, I just wanna thank you. Heck, that was some show you put on there. You saved my ass.'

The one with the Elvis hair gave me a big old Ronald Macdonald grin. 'It was our pleasure, kid. We all know what it's like to get picked on, but we don't take any shit from dudes like that no more and you shouldn't neither.'

They cheered and high-fived each other, holding up their little hands so I could do the same. I walked down the aisle, slapping palms and suddenly I felt myself getting tearful again, even though I felt better than I had all day. The last one must have seen my eyes, cause he held onto my hand.

'No need to get emotional, son,' he said. 'You'd have done the same, hey?'

I nodded. 'Too right I would, of course, no question about it.'

But I let go of his hand real quick and hurried past him back to my seat, before he noticed I couldn't look him straight in the eye.

Lost and Found

Rachel Crowther

A year ago today I lost my favourite handbag and found my husband. It seemed a fair exchange at the time, though not what I was expecting.

I'd left the handbag on a train. It didn't have much in it: my purse, my keys and my little leather diary were all in the pockets of my coat, because I didn't want to wear out the clasp on the bag by opening and closing it too often. But this made me more annoyed about losing it. I felt I hadn't made the best of it while I still had it.

I went to the lost property desk at the station the next evening without much hope of success. I'm the sort of person who can't leave stones unturned, however, and you could say that was lucky, because it turned out the man in front of me in the queue, hoping to find his umbrella, was my husband.

Not a new husband, you understand: it wasn't a case of love at first sight over the Network Southeast claim forms. No, it was my old husband. Michael. The husband I'd always had, at least until the day five years ago when he'd walked out—for good, I'd assumed—with no warning and no forwarding address.

It was an odd place to meet again, but it reminded me that we had things in common. Neither of us would dream of letting a lost umbrella go without at least filling in a form to record our regret at mislaying it. But then neither of us usually lost things. We were not careless people. Rather the opposite, in fact, which made it all the more surprising that we had managed to lose each other.

I knew as soon as I saw him that he would come back. I recognised his shoulders first, as he stood there patiently in the queue, and I thought, that's it: I might as well get used to that sight again. It could have been romantic, but it wasn't. We didn't bother with preliminaries, let alone a candlelit meal where we could spin a story to cover any awkwardness either of us might feel. We had a cup of coffee in the station café and he told me exactly how he'd lost his umbrella, and then he came home with me and we took up where we'd left off.

I never asked what he'd done during those years, because it was clear that he'd done much the same as before. Much the same as he went on doing. He still had the same routine, still kept the same hours. If he'd had another woman during that time she hadn't given him any new ideas, any tastes I didn't recognise. I was glad to have him back: it was better than growing old alone.

My life had been different since he left. Two distinct parts: with-Michael and without-Michael. Except that there were more parts than that: there was before-Michael, too, and now there was back-with-Michael. The funny thing was that I couldn't distinguish the parts as well as I expected. Surprisingly quickly, the with-Michael bits began to fuse together, and the bit in between melted back into the years before I'd known him. Sometimes he'd even drift into memories from those times too, as if it was too difficult to remember I'd had a life without him.

This was convenient, on the whole. It didn't occur to him that I might not be the same person as before, so I was. And there were things in those five years I was happy to give up: things that could be altered for the better by his presence.

So if you'd asked me yesterday, I'd have said it had been a success, resuming our old life, no questions asked. I'd have said, better the devil you know; we get along well enough, all things considered. But that was before the man in the shiny grey shirt turned up on the doorstep this morning with a smile I knew at once meant trouble.

'Mrs Ward?' he asked, the way people do when they know perfectly well it must be you. I shook his hand, which felt a bit clammy. One thing you could say for Michael, his hands were always warm.

'I'm from the church,' he said. 'From St Cuthbert's. Could I come in? I was hoping to have a chat.'

I made him a cup of coffee.

'It's rather a delicate matter,' he said. 'The thing is we're expanding. We have a flourishing congregation and we need more space. We've almost reached our fund-raising target now, so we've started thinking about the practicalities.'

He stopped to slurp coffee, even though it was still too hot. Not money, then, I thought. That was a relief, at least: I had a suspicion he knew exactly how much I had in the bank.

'The trouble is that we'll need to rearrange the churchyard a bit. Obviously we'll keep the disruption to a minimum, but it will mean moving a few graves. Especially the more recent ones, I'm afraid, because a lot of them are very close to the church. Including your husband's.'

'My husband's grave?'

He nodded. I imagine he was glad I'd understood first time around. Not that I had, really.

'You're going to move his grave? I'm not sure I like that idea.'

'Of course you don't,' he sympathised. 'People like their loved ones to rest in peace.'

I don't, I thought. I've got rather used to having him around the house again. If they move him, who knows how long it might be before we both wind up at the lost property office again?

I was in a quandary when he left. Several quandaries, in fact. The church was consulting all affected relatives, Grey Shirt had reassured me, but what about the inhabitants of the graves themselves? Was that my job?

The thing was, Michael and I had glossed over the fact that he was dead. It didn't seem to make much difference in practice, but he was bound to be a bit sensitive about it, especially a man like Michael who liked things to be straightforward. He might take offence if I mentioned it now, but I didn't see how I could avoid it. It wasn't something I knew anything about, his grave. I had no idea what part it played in his life—or should I say his death? Would it matter if they moved it? Would it hurt his feelings? Or worse?

Besides, I wasn't sure about the etiquette of our situation. What if Michael was only allowed to stay as long as I went along with the illusion that nothing had changed? What if he was obliged to go back, now this had happened, and he wanted me to go with him, wherever it was? I didn't mind having him here, but to be honest I wasn't sure he was worth that sacrifice. I wasn't in any hurry to leave, myself.

It was a facer, no two ways about it, and I couldn't think where to go for advice. It had occurred to me, just for a moment, to tell Grey Shirt about Michael coming back, but that smile told me it wasn't a good idea. It was an evangelical smile, and evangelicals don't like ghosts. They like people to be neatly arranged in heaven or hell, to stay put. He might have tried a bit of exorcism, and how would I ever have explained that to Michael?

I remembered then that I'd planned a little celebration for the evening, to mark a year back together. We didn't go in for much fuss, Michael and me, but he'd always liked a nice steak, and I'd collected the first windfalls from the garden that morning to make a crumble. I peeled the apples and chopped the carrots while I thought about what to do.

Maybe the casual approach would be best. 'Have you heard they're extending St Cuthbert's? Lots of people going there these days, appar-ently.' Or perhaps I should act as though I'd known all along—which I had, of course. 'I've never asked, Michael, but do you spend much time in your grave? It wasn't easy to get you buried there, you know. Marjorie from down the road helped: she was a churchwarden then. She's dead herself, now, of course.'

It was past the time he usually got in by now. I'd peeled a mountain of apples and got the steak ready in the pan, and I'd had a little taste of the wine I'd bought too, to help my thought processes.

When it got to nine o'clock I knew something was up. He'd always kept regular hours, Michael. Apart from the day he didn't come home, of course, and then there was a reasonable explanation. He was under the train instead of on it, that evening, through no fault of his own. But now he was dead that was one thing I didn't have to worry about.

I stopped when I got half way down the bottle of wine and wandered around the house instead. The odd thing was that I couldn't find a single thing that belonged to Michael. Not a sock, not a tie, not a stray button from his overcoat. It was as if he'd never been here; not since he died, anyway. I was feeling a bit woozy from the wine by now, but try as I might, I couldn't remember what he'd brought back with him after I found him at the lost property desk. He'd certainly travelled light, but surely not everything he owned was in the briefcase he'd carried off to work as usual this morning?

I didn't know where to start, looking for a dead man. The police would just have laughed. I didn't like to ring his office, either, in case they thought I'd gone mad. Had he really been going there every day, this last year? And the five before? Or had he stayed dead, as far as they were concerned? I wished I'd asked him a few more questions, now. But it was so restful, just picking up where we'd left off. I hadn't wanted to get into deep water.

In the end I decided to walk to St Cuthbert's. At least that was one place I knew I could find him. It was dark by now, but I've never been afraid of the dark and I knew the way. Up until a year ago I'd visited his grave regularly.

I hadn't bargained on running into Grey Shirt. He'd been at a meeting, by the look of it: other people were walking away from the church, and there he was, surveying the graveyard. Imagining how the new building would look, no doubt.

'Mrs Ward!' he said. Evangelicals are good at names: I certainly hadn't taken his on board. But he sounded pleased to see me. Perhaps that was why I decided to plunge in.

'The thing is,' I began, 'that my husband—he's been with me, this last year. He's been around a lot, and now he seems to have disappeared again. Since you came to see me this morning.'

Grey Shirt nodded thoughtfully. 'How long has he been dead now?'

'Six years.'

'Six years is a long time to be on your own, isn't it? I wonder—do you have friends who come to church, Mrs Ward? We're a very friendly lot, you'll find.'

I stared at him for a moment, then I started laughing. Rather rudely, probably, but I didn't care. 'Thank you,' I said. 'I'll certainly think about it.'

When I came round the corner I knew what I was going to see, and I remembered, all of a sudden, what it was like to feel happy, really properly happy. Sure enough, there was Michael, waiting on the doorstep. He must have forgotten his key.

Background

The 'story' competition this year attracted just over 400 entries, from which a short-list of 25 was drawn up for the judge, Susie Maguire. Susie is author of short-story collections *The Short Hello* (2000), *Furthermore* (2005) as well as editor of 4 short story anthologies. Over 20 of her own stories have been broadcast on radio. Here's what she had to say about the winners:

First: *Seeing Anyone* (Tom Vowler)
This was the most completely realised of the stories. Despite some reservations about the symbolic use of the dog, it moved me. The tone is right, the interaction emotionally powerful. Honest, sad, but beautiful too. The writer asks resonant questions about the death of a relationship, in a way which contrasts internal thoughts with external behaviour very sensitively. The fragility of the encounter is carefully composed, the language is reflective, subtle and sometimes poetic. The writer could have gone even further with it, pushed the dog-story, but the arc from anticipation to the final goodbye is complete here, and even after reading many other stories, it remains in the mind.

Second: *Wrong Bus* (Jo Field)
Like the first-prize winner, this story demonstrates the differences between a character's desires or intentions and their actual behaviour. Here, it's the gradual change in the central character from his interest in the glimpsed profile of a young woman to obsession and stalking, and then a final and ambivalent gesture. We are in the skin of (and can feel sympathy for) the character until almost the end, and I liked the way the writer shows the man looking for signs confirming his delusion. Though the pace is slow, it builds momentum nicely and has a haunting, cinematic quality, especially in the final few nail-biting 'frames'.

Third: *The Hour* (Hannah Eiseman-Renyard)
This story is funny and pacy right from the start, each sentence carefully pruned to enhance the sensation of things moving at speed; a confidently written piece of work. Again, it has a strong visual quality, could make a great short film. Because of the format and the gradual revelation of the

concept, by the end you want to re-read immediately to see if it might turn out differently. The characterisation of the protagonist and his motives are somewhat two-dimensional, but it's an entertaining gallop.

Commended stories:

***In the Constitution* (Joel Willans)**
I relished the sheer energy in the narrator's telling of this politically incorrect tale, which carries the brief action very satisfyingly, and with an instantly believable voice; and the final lines made me laugh out loud—ha!

***Lost and Found* (Rachel Crowther)**
Thoughtful, quietly amusing, and well-written, this is a ghostly love-story, surreal and tender.

~Susie Maguire, April 2008